Crazy Wheels

Written by Ann-Marie Parker

This bike has one wheel
and a seat.
People can ride this bike
by making the wheel
go around.

unicycle

This wheel goes
around and around.
This woman is making
the wheel go around
with her foot.
She is making thread.

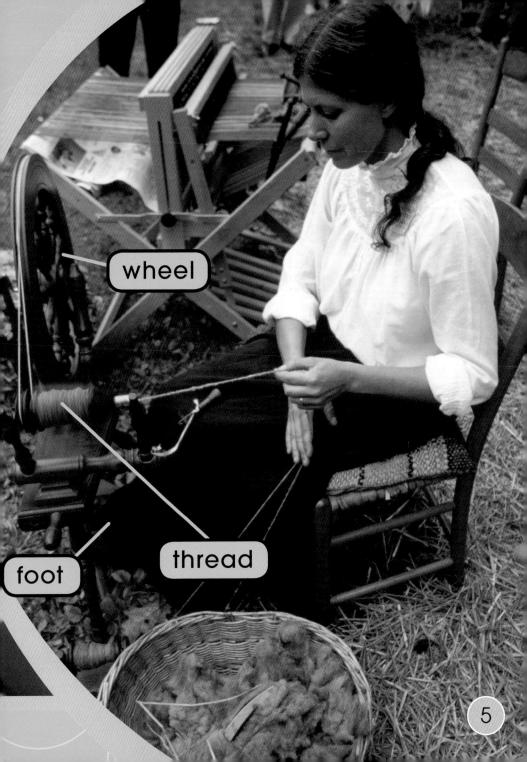

wheel

foot

thread

5

This wheel goes
around and around, too.
People get on the wheel
and go for a ride.
When people are on this wheel,
they can see far away.

Ferris wheel

This boat has
a wheel on it.
A motor makes the wheel go
around in the water.
When the wheel goes around,
the boat moves.

wheel

The water makes
this wheel go around.
It falls onto the wheel.
The wheel makes
a motor go.

water wheel

This wheel helps catch fish.
The water makes
the wheel go around.
The fish swim into a net.
The wheel lifts the fish up,
and they fall into the box.

net

fish wheel

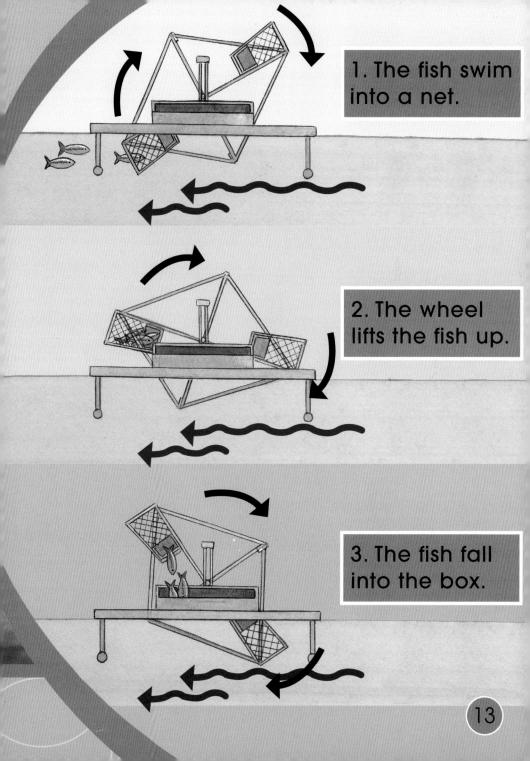

1. The fish swim into a net.

2. The wheel lifts the fish up.

3. The fish fall into the box.

13

Some animals
have wheels!

This turtle can't walk,
so a vet put wheels on it.
The wheels help it
walk again.

turtle

Index

Guide Notes

Title: **Crazy Wheels**
Stage: Early (3) – Blue

Genre: Nonfiction
Approach: Guided Reading
Processes: Thinking Critically, Exploring Language, Processing Information
Written and Visual Focus: Photographs (static images), Index, Labels, Captions, Diagrams
Word Count: 163

THINKING CRITICALLY
(sample questions)

- Look at the front cover and the title. Ask the children what they know about wheels.
- Look at the title and read it to the children.
- Focus the children's attention on the index. Ask: "What are you going to learn about in this book?"
- If you want to find out about a wheel that makes a motor go, which page would you look on?
- If you want to find out about a wheel that makes thread, which page would you look on?
- Look at pages 2 and 3. How do you think the people could make this bike stop?
- Look at page 14. What do you think could have happened to the turtle's legs?

EXPLORING LANGUAGE

Terminology
Title, cover, photographs, author, photographers

Vocabulary
Interest words: wheel, thread, Ferris wheel, motor, turtle
High-frequency words: making, around, so
Positional words: on, around, into, up, onto, in
Compound words: into, onto

Print Conventions
Capital letter for sentence beginnings, periods, commas, exclamation mark